ALL REZ

Hi, School

By Kalin Miles

Dedicated to my loving family, friends and frybread.

Chapter I: Hi, School

I pulled on the door, but it wouldn't budge until someone next to me pushed it open. *Good Job, me*. The day starts like the rest—a bunch of kids with disheveled hair and an alarming amount of ponytails shove their way into Fort Defiance High School. Of course, we do it begrudgingly, but honestly, we have nothing better to do. My name is Rita and I'm a Junior in high school. My mom got the name from some singer who she hoped I would grow up to be. I'm 15 so give me a few more years, some singing lessons, and a lil' plastic surgery, and I'll be all she dreamed I would be! Just as I entered the building, a familiar face approached me.

"Omg, Fritas, did you see the fight?" my *bestest of friends* Nizhoni asked.

"I wouldn't really call it a fight…I think the door won. They should really label it push." I responded.

We started walking toward the cafeteria.

"Yeah, that was kinda sad, but I mean the one between Johnny Jr. and John." Nizhoni said with a noticeable amount of enthusiasm.

"You sound happy they fought. I thought they were best friends?" I asked.

We sat down at a booth in the cafeteria instead of lining up for breakfast, because God forbid that we pretend what they serve is edible. Nizhoni fidgeted with excitement and recanted the tale as if it were some sacred oral tradition or folklore instead of a scuffle that happened 5 minutes ago in front of a vending machine. It doesn't help that the setting of the fight was underneath a decrepit roof that could collapse at any given moment.

"Well, apparently, John and Johnny Jr. have a crush on Samantha Redhorse, and I think Johnny Jr. and Samantha share the same first clan, but Samantha's first 3 clans are the same so I don't think that's really a problem—anyways, Johnny Jr. told Samantha that John was gay, then Johnny Jr. asked Samantha out but she said no to Johnny Jr., which I would too, but Naataani asked out Samantha later and she said yes, then John heard about what Johnny Jr. said about him being gay and they got in a big argument and started punching each other, but I don't think that's why they got in trouble; I think they hit the vending machine in the middle of their fight...also is John actually gay?"

She took a deep breath after telling me ten different things about ten different people I don't really know. Honestly, I was kind of overwhelmed by the information she had unloaded on me that took place over the past week and culminated in a fight that happened shortly before I got to school.

Before I could ask any clarifying questions and process anything Nizhoni spewed at me, her boyfriend Riley sat down next to her. I won't describe the PDA that ensued because this is a public space and a house of the lord. Okay, the latter part isn't true, but I will skip the description anyway.

"Did you have any classes wi—" is all I managed to say before being interrupted by Riley.

"Babe, come on, I want to see my friends."

"Ok." Nizhoni said with a tone somewhere between reluctance and relinquishment.

Both began walking away and toward a different cafeteria table. Nizhoni always acts differently with Riley. *She's quieter.* Which is a good thing for my ears and sanity. When she's not with him, she can talk about how much she loves him for hours. This is something I've caught onto recently; they've only been dating for a few months. I think it's a good thing; I mean, I barely know the dude. I met Riley in Biology last year when he asked for my Instagram and if I smoke. I said no to both, but he found my Instagram anyway and *tried* to *get me to smoke*. I ignored him so he ignores me now. Pretty poetic if you ask me.

I glanced around the cafeteria and saw all the many tired eyes burdened by their alarms ringing at 6 a.m. Most of us tiredly talked to our friends. Some of us begin our days in the cafeteria actually eating. *Imagine.* I like to scope out the cafeteria in the morning to see the many faces I grew up with and try to read them the best I can. People watching is one of my fortes; I've stared at people in the cafeteria during the early hours of the day since Creator created cafeterias. There's something more raw and truthful about Rez kids eating school breakfast than when they're in Biology pretending to care about amoebas and atoms. I like to read people based on their eyes—I don't see them as windows to the soul, but a reflection of what people have been dealing with. For example, some people are burdened and their eyes sink to the floor and some people's eyes are *too* upright and compensating for something; I respect the former a lot more. I'd like to think of mine as somewhere between the two. A good compromise of stress and strength.

600 Navajo kids. 500 with hopes and dreams. 400 with jet black hair. 300 girls. 300 guys. 200 kids with attitude. 100 people who I've never crossed paths with.

All in 1 high school.

We've all just got our cafeteria tables in the early mornings to talk about the gossip like we usually do or whatever Youtube celebrity's career is in the toilet. I don't have TikTok so you won't hear about that from me, but everyone else does so it must be important. I think we'd all be surprised about the different stories of the people we grew up with. Are they true? Do we care? *Should we care?*

I'd like to say *yes* to all three questions.

It keeps things interesting.

Ring. Ring. Ring.

The bell rang and most of us headed toward our home periods. Meanwhile, I saw Nizhoni and Riley discreetly head toward an exit.

Chapter II: Class Acts

For my home period, I have Mr. Howler. Mr. Howler isn't too bad; he's a mix of white savior with caring teacher. *Could be worse.* He's definitely an upgrade from the long-term substitute teacher I had last year who thought flirting was teaching... After morning announcements, Mr. Howler likes to do anything but teach. If I have a talent for reading people, Mr. Howler has a way with words, because they won't stop coming out of him. *Him and Nizhoni would get along great.*

"Hey, everyone! I hope we all had a wonderful weekend. Is anyone going to catch the Gallup parade? I think it's so cool!"

Of course, we are, but I'm not weird so I just stared blankly at Mr. Howler like the rest of the class. He should know better by now.

"I see we're all tired! No worries. Let's stand up real quick for a nice stretch."

At a certain point you have to give into his demands; we can only handle *so much* pity at a time. The class stood up and we stretched for about two minutes before we were rudely interrupted by

John being escorted by a security guard into the class. Poor dude, he had a bruise on his cheek, which is a lot less mysterious and less appealing than black eyes. I felt worse for his eyes that were sinking into his skull. His eyes were somehow retreating and avoidant, making it difficult to discern emotions that weren't melancholic.

"I'll take it from here, Officer." Mr. Howler said.

"I'm a security guard...," the security guard retorted as he pointed at his name tag.

"Oh, I know. It was a joke...," said Howler.

The security guard left without saying another word, and Howler began to pass out a cheat sheet for grammar. We sat down and stared at the piece of paper that had a pun about *"grammar and **me** being best friends."* Howler spent extra time at John's desk. I tried to eavesdrop...*what? You would too.* Nizhoni would be proud of me if she didn't play hooky today. I couldn't hear much of what they said though. I think Mr. Howler said that he was concerned for John. Also, John said that he was sorry. I also heard the word soup somewhere in their few minute chat, but I don't know where that fits given the context. Mr. Howler took long strides toward his desk, and John began to read his cheat sheet. His eyes weren't moving evenly across the page, nor did they seem focused on the cheat sheet. They were somewhat erratic and dejected. I could tell school was not his main focus at the moment.

John looked up, and looked directly at me. This doesn't really happen often, but he could tell I was staring at him. *I was in too deep.* I've never been the one to stutter nor too stunned to speak, but I didn't know what to do here. So, I gave a lil' wave. *Oh my god did I wave?* A part of me wanted to dissipate into thin air and evaporate like water. Another part of me wanted to cry myself to sleep in English class. Wait. *Did he just wave back?* I gave the best sly smirk I could muster before I turned back to my cheat sheet. *"If pronouns exist, do antinouns?"* Mr. Howler, I will jump you.

That small interaction with John went a lot better than I could've hoped. Worst case scenario, John thinks I'm a stalker who was admiring his battle scars, and the best-case scenario is he thinks I have glaucoma and can't control my staring. The rest of class went more smoothly and there were far less dramatics. I didn't stare at John again, but I think he stared at me. I know this because he did it a lot more conspicuously than I did. Maybe *he* has glaucoma? I just hope my face didn't look too much like a homeless chinchilla.

Ring. Ring. Ring.

"I'll see you at the parade!" Mr. Howler said before he began to reset as that was his talking point for the day.

I'll spare you the boring details of Chemistry and American History, but here are the highlights:

I have Samantha—Samantha Redhorse—in Chemistry during my second hour. She's a bit loud, but I can see what John and Johnny Jr. saw in her. She's really pretty, nice to your face, and funny; okay, she's not exactly a comedian but I laugh at her a lot. *Just not exactly with her.* I don't remember too much about what was taught in History, but we were talking about Lewis and Clark. Also, apparently Pocahontas saved a baby from a river, and someone said that she was their spirit animal... *I'm not going to address that.* I did however overhear Samantha talk about the fight between John and Johnny Jr. during Chemistry's individual reading time.

"Honestly, I'm not surprised... I mean, they kept asking me to hang with them at that new skate park Tony Hawk built. *Gross*. They're not as cute as my Naataani. Mhm. That's *my* chief. I didn't know John was gay though. What a w*aste*. But, it's none of my business" Samantha said to her friend Kay.

Let it be known here that I don't usually analyze girls. Their eyes do say so much more than boys', but they notice smaller subtleties and would catch me trying to read them. I guess that's just how it is being a girl—you read each other and hope for the best. I will however tell you that Samantha talked about the fight like some trophy of hers. I'm sure she got some pleasure over rejecting both guys and finding someone whose name translates to *'chief.'* However, I will say that Samantha has always been nice to me. I think it's because we barely see each other, and we never talk to each other.

"I mean. I don't know why John was so mad I found someone better. Naataani is a cowboy."

"I thought he was a bull rider," Kay said.

"Exactly. And he's super traditional. You should hear him speak Navajo. He sounds just like Mr. Begay." Samantha retorted.

"Mr. Begay? Our freshman year Navajo language teacher Mr. Begay?" Kay asked.

"Duh. Did you think I was talking about the substitute from last year who flirted with everyone? *Ick.* I bet Bailey's into that." Samantha said as she laughed with Kay.

"Ladies." Mrs. Scott said with a stern tone as she glared at the two with enough apathy to silence sheep on the butcher block.

"Sorry," Samantha said with a hint of annoyance as she puckered her face.

The two began to whisper.

"Wait, so why do you think John and Johnny Jr. fought anyway?" Kay asked.

"Don't tell Naataani, but I was messaging the two on Facebook and Instagram for months. Separately, of course, but they should've known better."

The two chuckled quietly but it was enough for Mrs. Scott to look up from her desk again, which was enough to signal to Samantha and Kay that they needed to be quiet for the rest of the class.

Ring. Ring. Ring.

American History was even less eventful.

I had Johnny Jr. in American History. He didn't say much. Actually, he didn't say anything at all. I did try to read him though. His eyes burrowed inward much like John's, but it wasn't in an introverted or shameful way. Johnny Jr.'s eyes were more secretive if that makes any sense. *If John was crushed by the fight, then Johnny Jr. was somehow stifled by it.* I would be too if I was rejected by my crush, attacked by a vending machine *and* placed on after school suspension because the principal didn't see enough to *actually* suspend me. And to top it all off—I look like a sheared sheep whose best friend is no longer my best friend, but instead someone I lost a fight to.

Ring. Ring. Ring.

Chapter III: Bone Apple Teeth

Lunch is really the only time I talk to anyone outside of the 11th grade. When Nizhoni decides to play hooky, I can't bring myself to eat alone at a table or in a bathroom stall like some movie cliché. I find myself entering autopilot, waiting in line for food, grabbing whatever gourmet slop is on the menu, and heading toward my favorite high school counselor's office. Mrs. Shirley is one of my favorite people—a short, frail woman with a personality that could stop an indicted Donald Trump in his tracks.

"Hey, Rita. Dr. Shirley is busy with someone." Rosa, the counselor secretary, said as I tried turning a locked knob on Shirley's door.

"Damn. I'm 0 for 2 in the door opening business." I responded.

"I saw that! Almost as entertaining as the basketball game against those Bordertown bastards in Gallup." Rosa said, basically crushing whatever little ego I had left.

I sat in the waiting area near Rosa's desk. Rosa's cool; she's very laid back and relaxed. I honestly wish I had her job as a counselor's assistant. She spends most of her days hiding her phone underneath her desk as she scrolls through Instagram, and she spends the rest of the day scrolling through Facebook. Luckily, she was doing just that as I started to eat my lunch. *Yum. Dry Turkey a la King.* I'm going to cry myself to sleep now, making today a relatively normal day. *I'm joking.* If you're going to take one thing away from this brief bonding with my inner workings, I'd hope it's that I'm pretty. But also, humor is *my* savior.

In walked another girl. It was Alexa Manygoats. She was a grade below me, really sweet and short. I think I could take her in a fight. Wait, I shouldn't measure people's body type based on if I think I could take them in a Navajo fight club. She looked sad, and it doesn't take a rocket scientist to figure that one out. Her eyes were red, and it looked like all of the tears dried around her eyelids. *Definitely not a pretty crier.*

"Sit down and wait one second. Dr. Shirley should be done soon." Rosa said while looking at her selfie camera. *Oooh, that's a good angle for her.*

"Ok." Alexa responded with just enough dejection that warrants a hello.

"Oh, hey Alexa. How's it going?" I said trying to assess if I can cheer her up in any way.

"Hi, Rita. It's going pretty good," she said with her eyes as red as a Colorado stoner's dream.

"Oh, are you sure? You look like something is bothering you." I responded.

"Yeah, just things…" she said, trying to avoid giving me any more details.

Well, can't say I tried. I met Alexa in a college prep program we both did for low-income students last summer. I think the Window Rock program was called Upward Bound but who knows. Two embezzlement scandals and some staff layoffs quickly led to it becoming *downward bound*. Back to Alexa. Generally, she is always bothered by something. She's usually on the brink of tears, but this is the first time I think she's let them out. There isn't much I can do.

I scoped the room, looking at how all three of us had such similar features. Jet black hair, dark eyes, and shorter builds. *Homogeny is the best policy?* I always forget about how much we all have in common. It's always a nice reminder that our commonalities only serve to accentuate our differences. I mean, it's intuitive that you throw a bunch of Navajos into one building, personality and our own sense of self is what defines our individuality. *Looks don't matter as much in that sense.* Sorry, I'm rambling. Let's get back to the mess that is the waiting room.

Mrs. Shirley's door swung open and woah did she look different. She grew 11 inches in height, gained 50 pounds and looked more Navajo than a medicine man. *Oh, wait.* That's Johnny Jr., and he looked the same. His eyes were still encumbered by the secrets he was withholding. I'm sure Mrs. Shirley tried to pull them out of the cage they lived in. Sadly, I think she failed.

Johnny Jr. scuffled out of the waiting room, leaving not a trace behind. There's not much for him to leave behind anyway. *I don't even think he wears a backpack to school.* Barely touched plate to the trash. Attitude ready. Time to spend quality time with my favorite counselor. Mrs. Shirley walked out of her office and said—

"Rita, you've been coming here a lot for lunch lately, and you didn't even bring lunch today."

"Well, I came to eat the words of wisdom you always feed me." I cleverly said.

"*Mhm*. Suck-up" Mrs. Shirley responded.

"Well, you're gonna have to wait one second. There's someone who I see more often than you. Hi, Alex."

"Hi, Shirley. I mean, Mrs. Shirley. Can we talk for a second? I swear it won't take too long" Alexa asked.

"Yes, Madam. Follow me." Mrs. Shirley said before Alexa quickly followed, shutting the door behind her.

Cool. Just me, Rosa, and her cellphone. That's all I need in this cruel, cruel world.

Usually, Mrs. Shirley takes a while to talk to whoever *actually needs her*. I usually don't, but she always insists I do. She also insists most people call her Dr., but she was my English teacher Sophomore year before she became certified to be a school counselor. So, we're basically friends. Also, she said that I've been here a lot more lately. Well, Nizhoni has been playing hooky a lot lately and leaving me to fend off the Rez dogs. *That tramp.* I hope she's doing her homework at least. It's one thing to leave me alone at lunch and it's an entirely different thing to drop out and leave me alone at school forever. Speaking of Nizhoni, she and *"Dr."* Shirley have a more strained relationship than I do with either of them. I really don't understand why, but it's always been like that. Despite that, Nizhoni has a better relationship than I ever could dream of having with Rosa; they follow each other on Instagram and are Facebook friends. *The betrayal!* Mrs. Shirley's door opened, and Alexa scurried off before I could say *'see ya'* or *'wear sunscreen every day.'* Mrs. Shirley turned to me and said with some level of dramatism as she beckoned me to enter her office:

"Come on in. We've got to talk."

Chapter IV: Therapy?

Mrs. Shirley and I had been looking at each other in silence for about a minute. We sat across a small desk covered in southwest trinkets and a mini cactus decorated as a Christmas tree. The only thing louder than the silence in the room was her Doctorate in Education from a barely accredited university in the Bahamas. The degree is framed and bordered with lights that hang behind her. This was honestly surprising because this was the longest that she's ever gone without talking. Sorry, Mrs. Shirley. *Or, Dr. Shirley?*

"So... what's new?" I asked.

"Nothing." She replied bluntly.

"I like the lights on your Doctorate." I said, calmly pointing toward the bordered frame surrounding it.

"Yeah, they change color," she said leaning back into her chair as she stared at me with an expression that insinuated I was harboring a wanted fugitive in my Jansport backpack.

"Lunch went by fast...we've only got 10 minutes left." I observed as I looked at the clock behind her next to a *Colonial Bros and Navajos* themed firefighter calendar.

"Have you been skipping class?" She finally asked.

I was a little shocked because I honestly never skip class. I'm too much of a chicken and there's nothing better to do than go to school. Am I supposed to walk 20 miles to Lotaburger and fight off rattlesnakes in late September weather? In the rural desert of Arizona?

"Um... well—" I articulated before I was interrupted by Shirley—the seemingly freelance detective.

"You're going to fail if you keep it up. You know better than that Rita! I can't believe you could be so careless and stupid. I thought you wanted a future? Why would you even come in here if you..."

I stopped listening to her speak. I scanned her room as she went on a tangent about how skipping school leads to drugs and becoming an alcoholic hobo otherwise known as a *"glonny."* The firefighter on her calendar for September's month is cute. I think he'd look even better if he weren't a white guy wearing a headdress from Spirit

Halloween. *Good for him*? She rambled for about three minutes before she picked up the phone and said—

"Now I've got to call your mom. Thank God your History teacher Mrs. Begay told me before you could spiral any further."

"I don't skip school. Also, I don't have Mrs. Begay for history. Also, can't you check my attendance?" I questioned, forcing her to put down the phone and log into her computer to look at my school attendance. Her hands stride over her keyboard when she types, and her clicks on her mouse sound like thunder. Her face changed from a light anger to a disappointed confusion.

"Well, I don't understand. She pointed at you this morning and said you've been leaving with your *friend*." She asserted.

She continued staring at my attendance, raising her eyebrows dramatically at one point.

"*Aha!* You haven't been going to Driver's Ed. I knew you were lying."

"As if Mr. Benally does his job." I retorted.

"I doubt he even knows how to take attendance." Mrs. Shirley nodded her head in a reluctant agreement. Which brought us both to the consensus that my name was cleared. Well, partially. She'll have to talk to Mr. Benally about doing his job.

"She seemed so adamant and worried. She pointed right at you when you were walking in the cafeteria this morning too. It was right after we laughed at you trying to open the door. She said that you've missed her class for nearly two weeks now and you're barely floating by. She even said it was because of your boyfriend. She said that if you missed one more week, you'll be held back and couldn't move up to the 12th grade."

"I don't even have a boyfriend..." I politely said.

"Figures. When you dress *like that*, that's what happens." Mrs. Shirley said with a tone of exasperation as she thought about who Mrs. Begay was pointing at.

I had to try to help Mrs. Shirley solve this mystery using my refined detective skills, which were cultivated in the finest of public schools in

Fort Defiance and St. Michaels, Arizona. Of course, I would help her despite the obvious shaming of my converse shoes and Beyoncé tour shirt. *Rude.*

"Are you sure she wasn't talking about Nizhoni?" I asked, knowing that Nizhoni would definitely be upset I nudged Mrs. Shirley toward her direction.

"I think it's Nizhoni!" Mrs. Shirley exclaimed with an excited tone that was a mix of *'eureka!'* and *'wow, I'm smart!'*

"I knew that Riley kid was no good. He didn't like the lights on my degree frame," she said as she quickly changed the color of the lights from a tame white to a slowly flashing Christmas theme.

"Can't make them go too fast... some kids have epilepsopsy."

"Do you mean epilepsy?" I asked.

"That's what I said." She responded with an assurance that I think Jesus Christ wished he had.

"So, what do you know about Nizhoni ditching class? Tell me more about Riley. You and him are best friends right?"

"Well—" I said just as the bell began to ring.

Ring. Ring. Ring.

"Crapola. Ok, you can tell me Monday," she said before she turned to fidget with her light-up Doctorate frame, burning one of the light bulbs to an empty darkness.

"Bich—" she said before she added onto it so it would not be a curse word.

"—on frisé."

She got that right. *Bichon frisé.*

The rest of my classes went smoothly, and I was off to home after the school day ended. If today taught me anything, it's that it was time to check in on Nizhoni.

Chapter V: 'O Clock

It's 5 o' clock now; that's the time I usually get home. I live in Saint Michaels, AZ, but it's next door to Window Rock. The bus ride home is always therapeutic. Just don't ask me about the number of times the bus feels like it's about to flip over because of how poorly maintained most of the roads in Window Rock and Saint Michaels are. *Those dirt roads make driving feel like a decrepit roller coaster in a Final Destination movie.* To give a timeline, school ends at 3:15 p.m., I wait for and ride the bus for an hour and 15-ish minutes, I get off the bus on my dirt road sometime around 4:45 p.m., I walk a couple unpaved streets down to Nizhoni's home from the bus stop, and if Nizhoni isn't at her house, I head home. This usually adds up to me getting home at 5 (give or take a handful of minutes). Today was unfortunately a day where her porchlight was off (that's how she lets me know to come inside); I had to head straight home to do homework. I wish I could tell you that I lived in a three-story Hogan with air conditioning, but I live in two trailers my grandpa connected and renovated before he passed away. Many won't call it a life of luxury, but we have running water and a microwave so *that's good enough for me.*

Most of the surrounding homes are wood and somewhat resemble traditional American suburbia, but we Sandovals didn't get the memo. Oh yeah, my last name is Sandoval. That's because my great grandma went to one of those Native American residential schools, and they made her change her entire name. She doesn't like talking about it. Well, let's get back to my Architectural Digest tour. We live on a singular acre, which is pretty small compared to everyone else on the unpaved block. The yard is a long rectangle with a gate that doesn't lock but we pretend it does. *Please don't tell the glonnys that.* There's one giant oak tree near the shed we use for storage, and there's a wall of tires opposite the house; to be honest, I don't really understand the purpose of the tire wall. Behind the wall of tires is an automobile graveyard with a broke down Ford van and a convertible car's frame that I'm going to guess is from the 60's. The automobile graveyard is also where we bury our beloved pets that got to meet Creator. So, it's actually just a graveyard.

The converted trailer itself is far in the back away from the gate; the shed is to its left, and the tire wall and attached graveyard is across. *Anyways, I'll wrap this up, but scenery is so deeply intertwined with all of our stories*. One of the best features of "the land" is a bridge we have that connects the tire wall over some type of DIY water canal that prevents flooding. I hope my low budget bridge to Terabithia paints a pretty picture of the promiseland my family is from. I completely skipped over the prairie dog camp that takes up a corner of the lot, mostly because I used it as target practice with a BB gun when I was in middle school. Just pretend you didn't read that last line and let's keep it moving.

I opened the door to an empty house, which is unsurprising. My mom and grandma usually get home past 9, which is pretty odd when you consider what normative work hours are. Their unconventional schedules make sense as my mom and grandma have unconventional career choices. My mom works whatever hours she can get her hands on at the funeral home up the street. I went with her to work one time and she used one of the bodies for a *"knock on wood for good luck"* joke. I personally didn't appreciate her making the lifeless hand of Mr. Tsosie knock on his own casket. *Maybe that joke will reach its target audience because it sure wasn't me.* I haven't been back to that funeral home since, and that was 8 years ago.

My grandma works in Fort Defiance at a nonprofit that hosts the Alcoholics Anonymous meetings. I call them family reunions, but my grandma made me stop saying that joke. *I relapse into telling it quite a bit.* I go with her to volunteer there when they host their meetings and especially during the potlucks. We don't call them potlucks when they're for Narcotics Anonymous meetings; it's *"not appropriate."* I disagree—potheads deserve potlucks! I think everyone needs to take the 12 steps to love handles. Overall, our three-bedroom trailer does us well. I always have the option to see my mom when she's at work, but I don't want to interrupt people grieving and risk getting run over by a hearse.

I set my backpack down by the door and hung my jacket up, then I went toward the dining room table with some papers and a pencil. This is the part where I do homework. I'm envious of you, yes—*you.* I have to do homework for a brief while and you get to skip that part of the story over entirely. *Rude.* If I have to suffer through Algebra II, then you should too. *But whatever.* I guess you're a guest in my story, so I'll be courteous. After solving some equations about y=mc squared and some triangle, I found myself thinking about Nizhoni. I knew she had been playing hooky from school, but she said it was only for her first hour elective study hall. She told me that she was always back before her second class started and I believed her. I wonder if her mom has any clue. She hangs out with her boyfriend and his friends during lunch, and they like to hide around. Either way, she never did this before Riley. I don't even know what they do when they skip school. Nobody was at her home when I walked over earlier and there was no way I was going to walk over again in a few hours. I guess all I can do now is video call her or wait until the parade in Gallup tomorrow. After doing my homework, browsing Facebook and Instagram, I checked the time.

Chapter VI: P.M.

In the top right corner my battery was a respectable 32% and the time was 6 p.m. My phone was shaking the table and an obnoxious ringtone played as I made the call to *Best Fran* on my outdated iPhone 8. Surprisingly, Nizhoni answered.

"Omg. Where have you been?" She asked.

"You're joking. I'm not the one who ditched class." I replied with a smug grin.

"Yeah, well, I had plans." Nizhoni said with some mystique and a wide smile.

"I think school counts as plans but I'm sure whatever you were doing was *so much more important*." I joked.

"Ah, Riley had this cute date planned for us. He bought me lunch and we broke into the abandoned middle school." She doted with Bambi eyes as she reminisced this afternoon...

"It was so romantic, and he said *it*."

"Said what?" I asked.

"He said he loved me." Nizhoni said with a smile that some might call *too* happy.

"It was so romantic, and he set up this picnic table in the abandoned cafeteria. Fritas, you should've been there."

"Sounds like I would've been interrupting." I responded.

"Yeah, you would have. But, it was so magical." She was full-on fawning. They've been dating for months but I don't think I've seen her happier. Actually, when McDonald's first made the Shamrock Shake, she might've been.

"Yeah, I'm going to have to pass on you and his *piccadilly willy*. So did you go back to school?" I asked, trying to transition to my concerns.

"Of course, silly goose! I was a little late but I'm sure I'll be fine." She said as her fawning turned into some moderate form of defensiveness. I could tell she was trying to play it cool.

"What about you Ms. Fritatas? Any lucky guy, *or girl?*" She asked as she chuckled.

"We both know I want to wait until college. I'm sure—" I said before being *rudely* interrupted.

"Sure, what? Miss out on all of the cowboys? Mr. Traditional? Fritas you can't save yourself for some lanky skater boy from Utah…" *Maybe, Nizhoni had a point.*

I stared blankly at the screen, mostly because Nizhoni made a relatively valid point, which I'm not too used to, particularly coming from her. She got me thinking that maybe I was missing out on something great. Was I waiting because I wanted to, or was I waiting because it was easier? Was it truly *for me?*

"I know that you're doing it because that's what your dad wanted. But, Fritas, you were 6. He was probably joking." Nizhoni said with some concern.

"It can't be that bad. I mean, Riley is amazing. What if you at least gave it a shot?"

Wow, Nizhoni was being persistent and forthright in her attempt to be persuasive, and I'm not even the McDonald's cashier she convinced to make her a Shamrock Shake in April. Sorry for bringing up the Shamrock shake—it's a big deal for Nizhoni. I heard rumbling around the background of the call coming from Nizhoni's side.

"God dammit! WHO TOUCHED **MY** LIGHTER?" The voice shouted in the background. Nizhoni looked behind her to see what chaos was unfolding.

"Nizhoni, did **you** touch my lighter? Don't act stupid. I know what kids your age is up to." The man in the background shouted.

"No, I didn't Johnny." Nizhoni said back in a quiet, respectful tone, which was abnormal for her. The Nizhoni I know would've been swinging her little arms and rammed her 5'1" body into the mystery man.

Nizhoni's mom has what one might call a "revolving door of men." Which makes sense because she works at our local grocery store called Bashas'. *She's all about customer satisfaction,* and what better place to meet people than the main grocery store in town?

"Well, some **dumb bitch** touched my lighter. *Aha!* It's right here by the TV. I didn't put it there. **Nizhoni**, do you know who put it there?" Johnny asked with a tone that insinuated Nizhoni had used it.

"No, I didn't." Nizhoni responded without turning around.

"Mhm. Well, when you see whoever did, tell them next time they **won't be so lucky**." Johnny said in a somewhat threatening manner.

Nizhoni''s bright and fawning eyes that were borderline worrisome quickly turned into ones with subtle fear.

"Um… I think I should go Rita." Nizhoni said to me quietly as her phone screen began shaking from her unstable grip.

"Wait, which Johnny is your mom seeing?" I asked just before she hung up on me and the screen went black.

Damn. I feel kind of bad for Nizhoni. Whenever her mom sees a man, she usually scurries him out of their home without Nizhoni seeing, and that's if he's even allowed into their home. Honestly, the only Johnny I know of isn't too great of a guy, and that's only because he always shows up in the Navajo Times for disorderly conduct and petty crime. Actually, I think he's Johnny Jr.'s father. They both have the rude and inconsiderate thing going for them, but it's a big, big Rez so I could easily be wrong.

This is around the time where I dig through the leftovers in the fridge. My grandma and mom always cook dinner absurdly late, so I'm forced to eat whatever their leftovers from yesterday are just to see the light of another day. I think they made frybread last night, so I'm especially excited today. I cleared the dining table of the disgusting garbage called *"math homework"* and put away my things before rummaging through the fridge for Navajo Taco stuff. *This gourmet living is something I can get used to.* With everything combined neatly on a plate, I put it in the microwave to cook. The rest of my night was rather uneventful—have you heard of Trisha Paytas? *Yeah, I didn't think so.* After catching up on all of the celebrity gossip, and spending hours losing my youth to Youtube and social media, my mother came home.

"Rita? Mother? Anyone home?" My mom shouted with her soft-spoken tone and slight rezzcent.

"Nope. Your daughter is roaming wild through the streets of Window Rock at 9 p.m. on a Friday night. And your mom is no longer hosting

A.A. meetings–she's joined them." I shouted back from my room.

"Oh, darn. Sounds just like them. I guess Rita won't be getting that new iPhone she's been asking for." She responded.

"I mean, I was joking, Rita is in her room studying hard and she's also going to find the cure for rheumatoid arthritis." I yelled back. As footsteps approached my bedroom door, I cleaned up my bed somewhat and changed the petty drama show on my laptop to act as if I was watching a Khan Academy math tutorial.

Knock. Knock.

My mother opened my door and took a step inside.

"Come in." I said in a snarky yet jovial tone.

"*Ha-ha*. Did you do your homework?"

"Nope. I did hardcore drugs like Doritos and Tapatio hot sauce instead." I responded.

She stared at me with a blank stare for a few seconds before I caved in.

"Yes, and I cleaned up a bit too."

"Good girl," she said proudly.

"Wanna hear tales from the funeral house?"

"Umm... do I have a choice?" I said with reluctance.

"No, but we can wait for your grandma to get home." She said.

I swear, if it's another joke about turning the funeral house into a funeral home...

We heard the door lock rumble briefly and the front door open.

"Rita? *Not Rita?* Anyone home?" My grandma shouted from the door as she hung her coat, purse and headscarf.

"Nope. Rita is lurking the streets of Window Rock for the finest of glonnys." My mom shouted back.

"Hey! I said I was roaming!" I yelled to clarify.

"And *'not Rita'* is at a decrepit bar in Gallup worse than Shalimar."

"It's Shalimar but *more*. Shalimore? I'll work on that joke."

We all laughed and began to migrate toward the living room. We then exchanged hugs, and I made sure to exchange some *looks of disgust* with my mother to keep her on her toes.

"We can't stay up too long tonight. We have the parade tomorrow." Grams said.

"Yeah, and no Youtube for you missy. Go to sleep by 10!" My mom said as Grams nodded with her in agreement. Both concerned I would stay up late.

"For your information, I fall asleep to Youtube! Also, you two need sleep more than me—it's 9:30, so don't even." I said with a joking attitude. Out all day and coming back this late at night! You two *prostitutes*."

I knew that was funny because it made Grams sarcastically scoff.

"So how was school Fritas? Did Nizhoni actually go today?" Grams asked as she tried to keep it lowkey that she knew more about Nizhoni than I did.

"What do you mean?" I asked.

"Well, I heard she's had an attendance problem lately." Grams replied as we all sank into our favorite seats, and she put up her hands to almost deflect my oncoming defensiveness.

"Mom... what happens in A.A. meetings, stays in A.A. meetings." My mom told Grams.

"Well, *I* don't count! I run them. It was also the poor girl's mom who brought her up..." Grams said.

"Sharice? I thought she was *too clean* and didn't need the meetings anymore." My mom said.

"Well, I did too but she always finds her way back to us. I hope Nizhoni is handling it well. Well, as well as she can when she's been skipping school. Maybe you should stay away from her Fritas." Grams said with concern.

"So, who wants to hear about the funeral house?" My mom said to change the topic in a rather abrupt manner to break the forthcoming awkwardness.

"Let me guess, you made the funeral house a *funeral home*." Grams said with her attitude.

"Damn it. I swear it's funny if you *let me* tell it." Mom replied.

"It wasn't funny the first time, and it probably never will be." Grams let off her chest

"What she said." I chimed in as I pointed at Grams.

"Ok so, today I met someone… and he asked me out." My mom said with some glee.

"Was he alive?" Grams asked.

"Mom!" my mom said as she hit Grams lightly.

"Well, ever since that knock, knock joke with the dead guy, I haven't had much faith with you." Grams responded.

"*Oooh.* I got the '*knock on wood*' joke." I said to Grams. Grams raised her eyebrows in disbelief of how many corpses my mom uses for jokes.

"Well, so both of you know. He was very much alive, and I've matured since both of those moments. We can all move on." My mom said in her defense.

"Yeah, to the *other side.*" Grams quipped.

"I also said yes, and we're going to the Gallup flea market tomorrow after the parade." Mom continued her news.

"And you can *embalm him* in your love." Grams said.

I laughed and had to give Grams a nice lil' high five for the cleverness.

"Good night my loves. This spring chicken happens to be 62, tired and not a chicken." Grams said as she began walking toward her room.

"Oh, and it's also not Spring."

"Night. Love y'all." Both mom and I said as we had a nice good night hug and walked toward our rooms.

"Rita, do me a favor and check on Nizhoni." Mom said as she turned from her door to mine.

"I will." I said as she dimmed the lights, and I pulled my door shut.

Chapter XII: Intertribal

The intertribal ceremony was pushed back to September this year because of COVID, but as always, it forces all of us to wake up at 6 a.m. and hurry out the door for a 45-minute drive to Gallup, New Mexico; yes, we were going through all this effort for a parade with Navajos, Pueblos, Apaches and even more Navajos. This *September heat* doesn't make it any more appealing, especially during the later hours of the day. If we get to Gallup before 7, we can get a breakfast burrito and a decent parking spot. If we get there after 7, we can get a breakfast burrito and a not-so-decent parking spot. We left Saint Michaels sometime around 6:15, I messaged Nizhoni, asking her where she'll be at the parade, and I asked her if we could meet up. I don't think she's awake now because I was left on delivered, and she responds quickly, *usually.*

The drive is pretty relaxing, but I wake up whenever the car hits a bump or sinks into the road, which we know by now is quite a lot on the Rez. Despite sleeping for most of the car ride, I did manage to enjoy the gorgeous red landscape of Arizona and New Mexico as we crossed state lines. The most beautiful gradient of red is the one you see in the Southwest desert of *'Murrica*. I grew up here, so I think I appreciate it more than most people. What you might see as barren land with no oil or prospect, I see as untamed with an unparalleled vivaciousness. The roadrunners run wild and the veins of Route 66 pump blood throughout the desert. It's a beauty you have to be keen for in order to appreciate.

Gallup is a border town, bordering reservations and insanity. Everyone treks to Gallup on the first of the month when their checks come in or for gatherings, such as powwows and rodeos. The Intertribal Ceremonial parade is a celebration of the cultural melting pot Gallup is, allowing all Natives to celebrate their heritage together. Some morons ruined the last celebration when they drove through the parade and had a high-speed police chase on what were closed streets. As you can tell, I'm very bitter about it. Hopefully, things go smoothly this year, and we can all bond over New Mexico green chili instead of fresh wounds and tire marks. Either way, I'm excited for the sparse free candy and the scary Apache clowns. Oh, look a sign: *Welcome to Gallup.*

My mom spent 20 minutes scoping downtown Gallup for a parking spot, which is surprising because 20 minutes is about how long it takes to see the entirety of the town.

"*ooooOoooOh.* That's a nice spot." My mom said as she gave a small opening between two cars her eagle eyes.

Just as she backed up to sneak her way into the spot, a giant blue truck cut her off and pulled into her spot.

"*AAaAAAAa!* That (*honk*)—ing b—(*honk*)" My mom said as she slammed her hands on the steering wheel.

"I think she's mad." Grams said to me with her ever so present sarcasm.

Mom gave Grams the side eye.

Out of what was practically a *monster truck* came a petite Native grandma with a headscarf.

"You're kidding me! That stupid b—" *honk.* Mom said as she harmonized with the car horn.

"Ok, we get it, can we find another spot?" I asked as the elderly woman turned from her *monster truck's* stairs.

"Is she…" my mom said as we all stared at this fragile brown woman with a cane give us the bird.

In sync we all returned the favor by throwing up one finger to show that the feeling was in fact mutual. The grandma seemed surprised we returned to sender.

"Well… it's just a parking spot, just pull into the one over there." Grams pointed to another spot slightly further away.

After pulling into the parking spot and getting out of our car, we passed the barrier into the parade's streets to find ourselves a nice spot to plant our lawn chairs. It wasn't too long for us to realize our parking fiasco cost us precious minutes and the only places we could sit were somewhat precarious. I personally did not want to plant my lawn chair on a broken storm drain. Grams suggested that we take the spot with a nice view on the train tracks, but mom and I quickly vetoed her suggestion. So, we walked along the crowded sidewalks for 15 minutes until we saw…

"Sharice! So good to see you." Grams said to our friendly neighbor.

"Howdy. I'm so excited!" Sharice said as her body contorted slightly with every syllable she spoke.

"Oh, yeah, meet Johnny." Sharice then directed us to a lanky figure that looked like he hated being there, hated her, and hated everything actually. He somehow smelled worse than he looked, exuding a pungent mix of *Bud Light* and tobacco. The only other notable qualities I can give about him are how soul-sucking his eyes looked and how malevolent everything about his person was. The dark brown pupils of his eyes were similar to a dark chasm that was pulling light into its darkness to extinguish it. His reputation speaks for itself; *he's far from a good guy.* Moreover, it doesn't help that Sharice's eyes were becoming more like his— absent of the motherly character I grew accustomed to, and absent of anything herself at all.

I didn't try to eavesdrop on the conversation between the adults; they were being especially boring, and Johnny had been steering Sharice away from the conversation with my mom and Grams. We planted our chairs next to Sharice and Johnny's in the prime spot along the sidewalk. There were two chairs that were empty with some things left unguarded. I don't want to speculate too much on whose belongings these are but it's a ragged purse and a skateboard. Two things I don't think I've ever seen one person have at once. *That's too much power and responsibility for one person if you ask me.*

"So, Sharice, how's Basha's?" My mom inquired.

"Oh, who cares? We're *here* now!" Sharice responded, continuing the weird contortions with her body as she puckered her lips to drink *"water"* from a paper bag.

"Oh, I was just wondering. How's Nizhoni?" My mom tried to continue her small-talk.

"That ungrateful brat? I don't know. You can ask her when you see her." Sharice said with a combative tone.

"Is she here?" my darling mother asked.

"Can you not? The parade is about to start. If I wanted to be interviewed, I would've gone to the Navajo Times." Sharice said, abruptly ending the conversion my mom initiated.

"She's around here somewhere. If you want to, you can go find her."

"I'll go look for her." I responded, receiving weird looks from Sharice and hopefully what is just her flavor of the week.

"It's starting. Try not to be gone too long. Look, there's already a banner." Grams said as she pointed her lips toward the First Peoples walking in the parade.

"I won't be gone too long." I said as I began walking down the sidewalk to scope the streets for Nizhoni.

Leaving the awkward scene of Sharice and her whole thing was probably for the best, but walking alongside the parade was an even more awkward setting. Instead of being able to enjoy the cultural meshing and celebration, I was now looking for Nizhoni. I let some of the parade pass me just so

I can catch the Apache clowns, embracing their healing and laughing at them scare the children nearby. *Classic. Or rather, traditional.* Gallup's downtown is a variety of jewelry shops with some restaurants mixed in. Food sounds so good right now. I forgot to hound my mom and grandma for a breakfast burrito, but we were too concerned with finding a good spot and jumping rude grandmas in order to watch the parade. *Grrrr.* My stomach decided to headline a concert at the parade, rumbling with hunger. Forget Nizhoni, it's time I get my priorities straight and find some good food. After making my way through the crowd of Natives, I finally came across a grandma with her signature headscarf and a water-cooler.

$3.00 for a breakfast burrito her sign read.

I gave a nice greeting and asked for a breakfast burrito with what I hope was a polite please.

"Sorry, I have no more. Let me call my grandson. He's about your age." The grandma said in response.

"John!"

"John!"

"I'm coming!" A slightly muffled voice said from inside the van the grandma was operating out of.

Out emerged a somewhat familiar face in unfamiliar circumstances.

"Oh, hi Rita." John said, holding an array of burritos that I could only describe as heaven on Earth.

"Hi, John!" I said with too much upbeat positivity for a chance encounter.

"What did you want, Gramma?" John asked.

"I'm all out. Help her while I make some more." Gramma replied.

As gramma hobbled away with her cane and headscarf, I turned back to John to finish our transaction.

"So, enjoying the parade?" I asked.

"Huh. Oh, forgot. I was on tortilla duty." John replied.

"I was looking for Nizhoni. Glad to run into you with your burrito business." I said as a joke.

"You kid a lot, huh? Yeah, it doesn't look like a lot, but I help my gramma whenever I can." He replied.

"Oh, of course! I was just saying it's cool…" I said with awkward unease as I tried salvaging the conversation.

"So, can I get a breakfast burrito with eggs? I don't really like the ones with potatoes."

"Oh, me too. You can take this one. It's spam and eggs." John replied.

I began to reach in my leather wallet for cash bills. I even made a joke about if his 80-year-old gramma takes Apple Pay or Cashapp.

"You don't have to. I can cover this one."

"Oh, thanks a lot!" I cheerfully accepted because I was not going to let Creator down by not accepting this blessing.

"Yeah, I make a lot from helping gramma out. I'm sure she wouldn't mind if this one went missing." John said while politely smiling.

"Thanks, again. I'm going to keep searching for Nizhoni." I replied.

"You're looking for the one dating Riley, right? I saw them down the street by that one big wall painting of a bluebird." John shared this crucial information.

"Behind or next to the mural? The one by Taco Bell?" I asked.

"I can show you if you want. I'll just have to see if gramma is fine by herself for a lil' while." John said as he slid inside the van for a brief moment.

John emerged as quickly as he entered, opening the watercooler to leave a few burritos in. He opened the top, revealing dozens of burritos. Grams followed John to the front.

"Oh, um…" I said *very eloquently.*

John's cheeks turned red in embarrassment or a slight fluster, forcing him to shut the container and leave the van to help me find my missing friend. We left behind a beaming gramma to man her stand.

Chapter XIII: Parade

I followed John through the tight crowd of people, eating my darling breakfast burrito as we steadily paced toward the Taco Bell. Well, I think we're going to the Taco Bell; that's the only place with a bluebird mural I know of. Our walk was not eventful, but I did cherish seeing more of the parade and some adults fighting over candy. *We've all been there, right? Question mark?* Laughter is medicine, and I was laughing a lot. My journey with John would not have been possible if we had to cross the street—there was no way we could interrupt the Natives dancing beautifully down the parade path. *I would never dream of it.* The festivities were continuing and the parade, much like a river stream, continued in one direction until it met a delta; this delta being police cars and other tired acts. As we were nearing the Taco Bell, I could see Nizhoni shouting at Riley by a dumpster while a group of his friends were laughing. She was teary eyed and looked hurt more than anything else. I sped up and passed John, jogging toward the scene.

"You're acting crazy!" Riley shouted at Nizhoni.

"There you go again. Always gaslighting me!" Nizhoni responded.

Nizhoni's hurt was turning into anger, which you could tell by the little slaps that met Riley's arms, which were then followed by her weak attempt at punches. Riley was starting to become more visibly upset, which was only exacerbated by the two other guys he was with that were shouting things like *"she's got you now!"* and cheering *"Nizhoni! Nizhoni! Nizhoni!"*

I was closing in as Riley slapped Nizhoni and the cheers from his entourage began to become a dramatic *"oooH."* Nizhoni was visibly stunned and backed up as I finally reached the scene.

"What the hell is your problem?" I shouted at Riley ready to fight him as he towered over me.

"Ask her. I didn't do anything." Riley responded.

"You know what you did." Nizhoni responded in a tone of defeat and hurt. Her face was bruising, which was surprising as I don't think I've ever seen a slap bruise before. Riley towered over me, and he looked even angrier that I had stood between him and Nizhoni, and before he could decide what to do next, John ran between us.

"Hey." John said as he landed a blow on Riley's jaw.

Riley recoiled but was ready with his friends to take on John.

In reaction, I put my pepper spray to use and aimed for Riley's eyes. I sprayed it in the air to threaten his approaching gang. It worked wonders.

Riley yelled a not so endearing expletive as he fell toward the ground in tears, yelling more naughty verbiage. John began to help me steer Nizhoni toward the sidewalk and back to our families. We began walking away from Riley and his *backup dancers* that were laughing at Riley's reaction to the pepper spray. He was in a semi-fetal position on his knees, shielding his eyes from the world as the tears streamed toward the concrete. *Oh, the mural was at the Taco Bell!*

"Why would you do that!" Nizhoni yelled as we paced ourselves on the sidewalk behind the crowds.

Nizhoni was apparently more upset at John and me for saving her from a boxing match with her boyfriend than she was at Riley.

"What?" I asked in a surprised tone.

"We were just playing around. You didn't have to do that to him!" Nizhoni yelled as the parade thundered and concealed her hurt amongst the crowd.

"Nizhoni, you weren't—" I let out.

"All you do is ruin everything, Rita!" Nizhoni said angrily.

"Wha—" *Nizhoni has a talent for interrupting me.*

"Just because you can't find anyone doesn't mean you get to take your jealousy out on me!" Nizhoni said assuredly.

"Jealous? *Jealous?*" I laughed a bit at the assertion.

"Oh, right. I'm so jealous I don't have a boyfriend that hits me in front of his friends."

"Ok. You two should talk about this later." John remarked.

"You're just mad that anyone you find would leave you anyway." Nizhoni said, trying to provoke a fight.

We stopped walking and started glaring at each other behind some small businesses in the downtown area.

"Oh, just like your dad?" I replied.

John became a sort of buffer, stopping us from immediately lunging at each other.

"At least mine is alive." Nizhoni said with a small smirk.

"God. Shut up! Who cares what happened to your dads—*they're both gone.*" John said to de-escalate our catfight before it became physical.

"Now, can I please take you two back wherever you need to go?"

Defeated, I held my head low and walked alongside the two, searching for my mom and grandma or a bus of Apaches to jump in front of. Our walk felt like forever until we caught a glimpse of my mom and Grams with Sharice missing from the scene.

"Oh, girls! There you two are." Grams articulated when we got close enough to hear.

"Oh, my... Nizhoni! Are you ok?"

"You're crying and you've got a bruise on your face..."

"I'm alright. I just fell." Nizhoni said, trying to avoid any further questioning.

"Let me help you clean up. I have some face wipes." My mom offered.

"No, it's fine." Nizhoni declined just before sitting in the passenger seat of Sharice's Jeep and closing the door.

"Okay, well..." my mother said.

"So, Rita, who is your friend?" She asked, looking at John for an introduction or response. I think her sudden shift in conversation was to give things some order.

"Oh, umm... hi. I'm John." He said.

"I'm Rita's mom." My darlingest mother said as she shook his hand.

"And I'm grandma!" She exclaimed as she gave John a half-hearted hug that felt more like a diplomatic move than an endearing one.

"So what were you kids up to?" Grandma asked, trying to probe more into what happened to Nizhoni.

"Oh, we just got Nizhoni." John responded.

"Yeah, and she biffed it by the Taco Bell." I said, trying to explain the mysterious bruise.

"That's funny because the bruise looks like a handprint..." Grams said trying to pull something out of us.

"Well, that's just what Nizhoni told us." I said.

"Yeah, she had it when we found her." John contributed to the narrative, trying to bolster the credibility of our lie.

"Well, you two let me know if you hear a *different story.*" Grams said. She looked at both of us before going back to her lawn chair.

"I'm going to go back to my gramma now that you have yours. I think you have a lot to do here, too." John told me.

"Thanks, John. *I couldn't have walked to Taco Bell without you.*" I said, trying to lighten the mood.

John stared at me blankly.

"Joking. I'm just joking."

"Oh, well. I don't know if this is the right time to ask—" John was interrupted by a voice an octave lower than his.

"And **what the hell** is he doing here?" Johnny said with an undeniable animosity targeted toward John.

Johnny and his brilliantly named son Johnny Jr. were walking together to our makeshift parade site. I'm guessing that Johnny went looking for his son as I went looking for Nizhoni.

"Oh, yeah thanks for helping us out." I said trying to shoo John away to avoid any conflict.

John's face became stone cold and his demeanor intimidating.

"I don't need to know why you're here. Did momma kick you out again?" John said, looking for another fight.

Johnny Jr. tried to close in on John, extending his chest out and trying to escalate things. I was the only thing that stood between the two, acting as a barrier of sorts.

"I don't think either of you want this…" I said, trembling as the two stared at each other, waiting for one to make a move.

"Also, there are a bunch of cops." I pointed to the many Navajo Nation and Gallup police cars in sight.

Everyone was anxious—all parties within earshot had noticed the commotion. My mom and grandma were standing with Sharice, and Johnny was slowly creeping toward the two boys.

"That's enough." Big Johnny said to little Johnny. He pulled him by the shirt, trying to deescalate the scene. As this show began to climax, the parade's acts became noticeably fewer and fewer.

"Man, let go of me!" Johnny Jr. said, shoving his father's hands off of him.

As quickly as he pushed him off of him, Big Johnny punched his son, forcing his Jr. to fall to the ground.

"What the hell is wrong with you!" Grams let out.

"Don't tell me how to raise my own **God damn** son!" Johnny retaliated.

Of course, an officer started approaching, which was bound to happen with all of the yelling becoming the new parade.

"Is everything okay here folks?" The western cowboy dressed officer asked.

"Yes, officer. He just fell." Johnny said as he grabbed his son from the ground by the collar of his shirt.

"Right, Junior?"

"Yes." Johnny Jr. said in a defeated tone, simultaneously giving John a menacing glare instead of his father who knocked him to the ground.

"Alright. Be careful where you walk, son." The officer said as he continued to do his rounds.

Not too long passed by but that was enough for my mind to conceive many a thoughts. Should we have said something? Would that have made things worse? I don't think Grams could've handled a fight.

"Get in the car." Johnny said.

Johnny walked toward Sharice's ride, pulling his son along with him until they got in.

"Well, it was nice seeing you guys! Catch ya on the flipside!" Sharice said, mustering a smile that failed to conceal her fear and inner turmoil. She grabbed their things and lugged them into the trunk, throwing the lawn chairs into her Toyota. The scene was chaotic and Sharice's ability to throw and carry everything was superhuman. She would've been calmer if Johnny didn't honk the horn to hurry her.

"I should go back to my gramma." John said, angrily staring at the car.

"It was nice seeing you."

"You too, John." I said back to him.

As Sharice's car pulled away, so did John, and my family grabbed our chairs and headed back to our ride. I remember pondering the entire situation, which lasted the entire ride home. I was too preoccupied to think about anything else, but I do remember my mother getting off at the Gallup flea market for a date. The rest of the ride home with Grams was quiet.

IX: Good Mourning

Good morning and welcome back to *not the Kardashians*. It's been a couple of days since the parade. *What a mess.* I don't need to give a recap for Sunday as following that drama it was relatively boring. We didn't talk much about the incident. *We usually compartmentalize our emotions and fold them neatly onto our soul.* It's a lot easier to let things weigh us down than trying to intervene where we aren't wanted and risk becoming the target of others' wrath. Time heals, so let's just hope two days heals enough for everybody. My mom said that her date went amazing but I didn't get too many details as she was exhausted from what was apparently a 12-hour-long escapade. This Monday morning, I woke up at 6:00 for ample time to get ready for school and eat breakfast. The bus comes around 7 and takes its time to get me to school. School is so far out of the way for my mom and Grams that I never ask for a ride, and by the time I'm gone, they're just waking up. The only hard thing about riding the bus is passing the time. 'rEaD a BoOk' you say, but the potholes and dirt roads don't afford me that luxury. Also, this d*efinitely didn't* happen to me, but I heard somebody tried reading on the bus in middle school and puked out of the window from motion sickness. Of course, *I myself would never be in a situation that embarrassing. Haha.* But, live and learn, right? I can't even be an annoying teenager and go on my smartphone. Cell service is so spotchy on the Rez that trying to focus on a 5 inch screen in an unstable bus with no signal isn't worth it either. Also, *I heard (I can't stress it enough that this was heard)*, that a freshman tried it and got motion sickness then puked in her backpack. *It was her favorite red Jansport backpack, too.* Of course, these two instances are through-the-grapevine information. She really loved that backpack too. :(

Like clockwork, I finished eating my cereal and walked the acres from my front door to the bus stop. I've gotten really good at timing when the bus comes, so I only had to wait a few minutes. Steps onto the bus, then one seat near the back later, I realize I've taken little note of my surroundings on this fine September morning. Just trust that the traditionally red landscape is just as beautiful at sunrise as it is at sunset. I usually have this time to ponder life's deepest questions. *Will Beyoncé ever go on tour again? Is Kim Kardashian really going to become a lawyer? Why am I so mad at Nizhoni?* This morning's questions were asked in descending order of importance. I'll only try to understand my anger toward Nizhoni now for time's sake. We've fought before, but it was never over a guy. We've hurt each other's feelings, but never taken it this far. Was I in the wrong? No. *At least I hope not.* I never really liked Riley. He was rude and seemed apathetic toward everything. His humor sucks and his apathy is *suckier–h*e just sucks. Sucks the air out of the room. Sucks the sunlight from the blue sky. Sucks the life out of others, especially Nizhoni. Maybe I'm just bitter she's spent a lot more time with him than me since they've "fallen in love." *No.* I've been doing just fine without her, but of course we've strayed apart. What else was supposed to happen when she started seeing someone? I turned my head toward the window. The bus is dragging us along bumpy dirt roads as the sun creeps forward from behind the distant mountains in the backdrop. When I can't count on Nizhoni—at least I can always count on the sun rising.

I'm walking into school when I turn toward the cafeteria, and I see Nizhoni with her P.O.S. *handler* displaying enough P.D.A. for a Rated PG-13 theatrical release. *Gross.* I try to ignore her bruises that were poorly covered and blended with makeup *I gave her!* Oh, well. I think today I'll give my trusted guidance counselor *"Dr."* Shirley an early visit. I walked passed classmates that hovered between the halls and the cafeteria, entering the front office, exchanging greetings with everyone that I knew. I tried walking toward the counselors' offices, but saw Rosa before I could make it.

"Hey, Rita. Have a good weekend?" Rosa asked.

"Yeah, it was fine." I said, trying to mask my pain.

"That's good. Why are you in the office before school starts? Shouldn't you be *TokTok'ing* and on the *'gram?*" she said, confidently using fake lingo about social media.

"Um... I guess. I just wanted to say hi to Mrs. Shirley." I told her.

"Well, she's actually in a meeting with some school county people. I don't think it's going *lit.*"

She informed me. I'm not going to address her use of *'lit.'*

"Ah, okay. I'll just go *'toktok'* in the halls and wait for class to start." I told her before moving away to start waiting for the bell that herds everyone to class.

Ring. Ring. Ring.

'Twas the day before night. When all through the school, every creature was stirring, even that *tool* (Riley). Many pencils were brung and only some cared, but we'd all rushed to class, hoping to get there.

"Hey, class! Wasn't the parade great!" Mr. Howler projected to all of us.

Silence.

"Well, I can see how tired all of us are. Let's stretch."

We capitulated to his demands, being too tired to object. Just like every other morning. I did see John in class and this time he waved at me. I could tell he was happier and the weekend lightened the weight on his eyes. *I waved back.* We stretched for a short while before having to pledge

our allegiance to America, *including New Jersey.*
Gross. Mr. Howler passed out his usual worksheets
with bad puns. *'What's the hype—with 'hyphens?''*
and *'Question, Mark?'* At least the jokes are getting
better. I'm slightly embarrassed John had to witness
my problems over the weekend. We'd never
crossed paths before that. *Okay, that's a lie.* We've
had many classes together through the years, but
that can be said for most of my grade. Just because
we *know of* each other doesn't mean we *know* each
other. Nizhoni still weighed very heavily on my
mind. I was too busy thinking about what would
come next–*if anything.* I can't not do anything or
say anything. That'd be 16 years thrown away
because of some gross *thing* named 'Riley.' We did,
however, say things that I don't think we should
have. *But, why am I the one who always has to
reach out?* While in Mr. Howler's class, I realized
that I've been the one rebuilding every bridge
Nizhoni has set ablaze. It felt like I was her form of
damage control, repairing whatever she breaks with
her carelessness. I've made up my mind. Nizhoni
would have to fix things this time. Forgiveness is a
quality emblazoned in my consciousness, but this
time I've made up my mind. The rest of class was
fairly normal–much like all of my classes that day.
The outliers of that class were me and John meeting

eyes and smiling. Well, I tried to hide my smile, so it was more of a smirk.

Ring. Ring. Ring.

"Okay, see you all tomorrow!" Mr. Howler yelled across the classroom.

We all scurried toward the door, and I made note of John's eyes. They were regular looking, but they radiated a dark brown that expressed a giddiness I don't think I've seen too many times before. We met eyes again, and his curved with the smile he made. *Cute.* I stopped leaving with the huddle my peers formed when I thought I heard my name. John staggered a bit as if he was trying to match his pace with mine, but he moved on when I came to a complete stop. *I'll see you later John.*

"Rita!" Mr. Howler said, directing me toward him.

"Yeah?" I was confused as to why I was stopped. My tone and caught off guard demeanor conveyed just that.

"Oh, I'm sorry. I just wanted to see how you feel about *'everything.'*" Mr. Howler said.

"Um… I'm good with *'everything…'*" I replied with just as much confusion as before.

"Cool… I'm sorry that this is awkward. It's just such a small world. I wouldn't want to make things weird and if it bothers you… let me know." Mr. Howler informed me.

At this point, some students had arrived and they found their seats. Some had to walk right around us, trying not to disrupt whatever this conversation was.

"Yeah, *'everything'* is fine." I said, trying to conceal my confusion just to get this unexpected conversation to end.

"Okay, great! Now get to class. I'll see you around." Mr. Howler talked *without actually* letting me know what *'everything'* I was supposed to be *okay* with was.

I walked to my next class, and Samantha Redhorse was more distracting than usual. No matter how hard I tried to focus on chemicals or whatever Mrs. Scott was adamant would save the planet from Global Warming, my attention kept being interrupted by her gossiping. Sadly, I can only relay what I did hear. Apparently, someone posted really weird things on Instagram and Samantha's boyfriend said to "stay away" from whomever it was. I didn't hear who because Mrs. Scott said that whatever was on slide 3 would be on the test this Friday. I think it was Greta Gerwig and the Climate Crisis.

"Yeah, just, I don't know… please, don't try to bother him… it was scary but I don't really know what it means." Samantha Redhorse notified her lackey Kay but I sadly couldn't catch the rest until the tail end.

"Omg, I totally forgot. There was a g–"

Mrs. Scott shut down the conversation. Staring at the two girls with one of her signature blank stares.

"Now, Samantha. This is not a social studies class. I don't care what you get away with in Woodworking or Driver's Education—I should be the only one talking." She stated her conviction with a stern pose before returning to the powerpoint slides.

Ring. Ring. Ring.

I'm skipping over what was a very mundane class period. *Sorry, America, but not you New Jersey.* Well, I did notice that Johnny Jr. wasn't there today. Anyways...

Ring. Ring. Ring.

Everyone walked toward the cafeteria. I was walking and noticed that I went straight passed Nizhoni. I think that's for the best. I did imagine a fake conversation with Nizhoni where I was finally standing up for myself. It opened with something along the lines of *"Oh, hey. I'm so very deeply sorry you can't think of anyone else's feelings but yours. I would too if my boyfriend was just Mr. Prince Charming like Riley!"* That was the nicest thing I said in the fake conversation. I also said that I would yell her name 3 times at the next wolf I see as some sort of threat. *Thank you, maladaptive daydreaming.* My only viable option for lunch today is to go to the counselor's office. I'm not even going to bother getting in line for food. I set my course to the counselors' offices and was caught off guard when John approached me from behind.

"Oh, hi." John said as I turned to focus on him within my periphery view.

"Hi." I said back, stopping outside the front office door to talk.

"Are you getting lunch?" John inquired.

"No, I'm fasting." I joked.

"Oh, why? You're not *that much* bigger." John said.

"Oh, well. That was a joke." I said, slightly offended.

"Mine too." John said, chuckling at himself.

"Good one. Your gramma's burritos would be to blame anyway." I retorted.

"I think that's a good thing." John informed me.

"Okay, well, bye." I said, trying to abruptly end the conversation in order to wiggle my way into Shirley's office.

"Wait! What are you doing later?" John asked as I was about to move on.

"Probably crying to a YouTuber complaining about being rich tonight." I answered.

"Oh, that's kind of sad." John figured.

"That was funny, too." I said.

"What do you mean?" John said mildly confused, which told me he thought I was being completely serious this time.

"Oh, um... but if you're not busy, then we should hang. There's a new movie in that theater behind Bashas'. We should go."

"Oh, yeah sure. Sounds nice! What time?" I asked.

"Probably around 7. I was thinking we could watch the new *Barbie* movie. I'll message you on Snap. Just send me your address." John said to me.

"Cool. I'll pick you up." Then he walked away.

Huh. Is that a date? Oh, well... I don't really know how to feel. My stomach feels a little queasy and my palms themselves are shaking a bit. How does that even work? *How do I feel?* I think I feel happier than sad, which is nice because I've been in a rut since Saturday's parade. I just have to be home before 9 so mom and Grams won't interrogate me. I turned to open the office door, trying to push it open, but I think it's locked. Confused, I kept pushing.

"Rita... it's kind of sad at this point." Rosa observed.

"Oh, hi! Is the door locked?" I asked.

Rosa moved forward, looking at me the entire time and *pulled* the door open. We didn't say any more words, and both of us quietly took our seats by Mrs. Shirley's door. Rosa proceeded to go on what I think was TikTok. I'm taking a stab in the dark because it was a sped up song by Alvin and the Chipmunks, which was fast and extremely obnoxious. Oh, I lied. *It was just a Maroon 5 song.* I decided to go on my phone because I didn't even bring food to eat today. *Hmm.* I'll send John my address now just in case. As I was sending my address, Mrs. Shirley emerged from her room with Alexa. Alexa was beaming and gave me a nice wave when we made eye contact, which I reciprocated.

"Oh, see ya Rita!" Alexa said right before she left the room to the cafeteria.

"*Mhm.*" Mrs. Shirley reacted as she directed her attention at me and waved me into her room.

We took our seats and I decided to scope the room. Mrs. Shirley's office remained unchanged, making the awkward silence palpable. The Southwest decor still covered the room head t–

"*So*, did you eat lunch?" Mrs. Shirley asked.

"I didn't today." I replied.

"Good. Work on your outfits next." She immediately returned.

????

"Ok, now that Alex is gone we can discuss '*everything.*'"

"It's Alexa." I responded.

"I think I know my students better than you do, Rita. Well, that's not what I'm talking to you about today." Mrs. Shirley stated. I felt her stare intensify and her somewhat carefree aura become stern and inquisitive.

"You would know more about this than I do. I'm talking to her later, but with the truckload of foundation covering her neck and face, I don't think it'll help much." I think I know where this is headed, and to be fair–I don't know how to help her either.

"So, Nizhoni... a teacher pointed out a few bruises. Is Nizhoni doing alright at home?"

"Mrs. Shirley–" I said, being interrupted.

"Dr." Shirley rebuffed.

"Erm. Okay–*Dr.* Shirley."

Dr. Shirley nodded in an approving manner with the correction.

"She hasn't said anything to me, *personally."*

"Personally?" Mrs. Shirley said. Sorry, I meant *Dr.* Shirley.

"She seems fine to me." I lied.

"Really? Your best friend who looks like they've been dealing with crippling despondence and has a bruise *shaped like a handprint* is fine?" Dr. Shirley said with a tone of annoyance toward my response.

"Okay, did *you* hit her?" Her question changed.

"No, why would you even..." I said defensively.

"Why are you acting like this then?" Dr. Shirley said with an underlying tone of conviction.

"Because, nothing I say will be good enough for you." I responded.

"*This. Is. Not. About. Me.*" Dr. Shirley said, exasperated.

"This isn't about you either."

I'll admit. I started to feel really bad, but it wasn't my place to say anything. Nizhoni wasn't my problem, especially after everything she said to me.

"So that's it. Your *'supposed'* best friend is showing up with mystery bruises and you're protecting whoever did it." She accused me.

"No. That's not what that means at all!" I exclaimed.

I got up and grabbed my backpack.

"I don't know what you want, but it's not me you should be asking."

"No, sit do–" *Mrs.* Shirley said while I turned my back and left the office.

On my way out, it seemed that Rosa was trying to ignore what we were talking about as she vigorously typed on her phone and stared intensely at it.

Ring. Ring. Ring

Ring. Ring. Ring

Ring. Ring. Ring.

The school day flew by, and after what *I wish* was a short bus ride home, I was situated in my kitchen. *Somewhere is here, because it's 5 O' Clock.* I didn't bother seeing if Nizhoni's porch light was on today. I'm busy anyway, and if I wasn't–I still wouldn't want to see her. Tonight's to-do list is homework, Youtube, food, date, then bed. *Wait. Date?* I almost completely forgot because of how much Nizhoni has occupied my mind today. It's like an unwanted tenant in my mind's valuable real estate–she's a *squatter.* That's it. Nizhoni is a squatter, refusing to leave my head alone. She's been consuming my time and energy when I can devote it to more valuable pursuits, such as John. Okay, a guy I barely became acquainted with last week isn't more important. *Pertinent.* That's the better word. The hours are only dwindling between me and 7. I'll focus on my homework, which we know is usually disgusting math, so we'll move over that part of the story for your sake, *and for mine*.

At 6 P.M., I got ready, but honestly I didn't need to do much. I've never been high maintenance, which is a nicer way of saying that I'm lazy. I decided to check if John read my message, which met me with it showing I had been left on *Delivered*. At this point, nothing was alarming or worrying, because most of the movies start at 7:30 anyway. I'm sure he'll read my message in the coming minutes. I spent the next 15 minutes switching between Youtube videos and my messages to John. Every time I checked my phone, I was met with a *Delivered*. I relinquished my care to the wind and fell into a Youtube conspiracy hole, spending the next half hour on whether or not TikTok was selling our data to foreign countries. *Oooh. That's almost scary.* I checked my phone sometime around 6:50 to see that there were no new notifications. However, my message was now marked as *Seen*. I figured he'd be here soon. Sadly, I was wrong. He never came, and I went to bed angry, annoyed and dejected. The hours only kept piling on after 7 that evening, and I couldn't really muster an appetite. I didn't tell my mom or Grams what happened, because I don't know what happened either.

The sun rose the next day, and nothing seemed different about what *was yesterday's tomorrow*. I woke up surprisingly calm despite being stood up, and continued with my day. Finding myself in Mr. Howler's room for home period. I remember the room looking the same–all of the familiar faces were there but one. Truth be told, the next two weeks felt like a collage of different moments. I remember hearing the announcements, carrying on through class normally. I remember Mr. Howler said his usual quirky jokes about punctuation and grammar. Samantha Redhorse talked as much that day, Dr. Shirley asked if I "needed anything." She chased me out of her office for *"people who actually needed her."* Alexa was crying. I went through the motions of the day, preparing to do the same for the next, but everything had come to a head. The very next day felt like an inversion of the previous. Mr. Howler didn't make any jokes. Samantha was quiet. Dr. Shirley still chased me away when I said *"I didn't know him that well."* Alexa was crying again, but I don't know if it was for the same reason I wanted to. My memory of the next few weeks is cloudy, being over encumbered by a growing sadness. I remember the end of September and beginning of October as a collage better than a continuous story.

The funeral was nice. My mom did a lot of the work and it was the first time I had been there in many years. I remember hugging his gramma. Mom told me Johnny Jr. used a gun that his dad wasn't allowed to have because of his probation. *Both Johnnys went to jail.* I cried when no one was around, because it felt selfish to feel sad for someone I didn't know all too well. Nobody needed to know about our brief friendship. Maybe it was selfish to hoard the memories, but it felt nice knowing I had something to hold on to. The worst part of '*everything*' is that the world looked the same—no matter how big the tragedy, it felt like everything was still moving. I didn't *just* care if people moved on. The simple act of moving bothered me. I felt stagnant and stuck in one place, watching everyone have the audacity to *'move.'* The sun rising and setting upset me just as much—it felt like it wanted to separate me from something I didn't want to move on from. I tried to avoid *what if's* and my own speculation because I knew I couldn't change what happened. Those three weeks escaped me. Just like he did. I was caught in a low light, wading through what felt like treacherous waters, trying to grasp air itself to use as a lifeboat when I found myself submerged in melancholy. *Which was a lot of the time.* That Monday was the last time I saw John.

X: Ex

Oh, hello. I forgot I was narrating my life. These last few weeks weren't my best. I kept going through a cycle of frustration, anguish and resentment. My grades weren't slipping, but my mask was. I was just pushing through the days and a few people noticed. My Grams, Mr. Howler and Mom. Mom and Grams offered the same support but I didn't tell them anything other than that it was just sad that someone I knew was gone. I didn't tell them anything else. I remember being angry when Grams said Sharice spent the entirety of an A.A. meeting sobbing about losing *"the love of her life."* Sure Sharice, Johnny being in jail for owning a gun is so much worse than being in front of its chamber. I don't even want to talk about the person who held it. Which is why I've exerted so much effort to avoid the paper, Facebook tributes and any other social media, really. *Ignorance is my only bliss at the moment*. Mr. Howler was a lot nicer than he should have been. He canceled a test and we watched a movie. He put on the 2000's classic *White Chicks* but he made us keep that a secret because he forgot to give us a waiver form. We talked a little bit and it went something like this:

"Did you know him well?" Mr. Howler asked.

"No, but we were friends." I responded.

"I'm so very deeply sorry. Here, take this..." Mr. Howler told me as he handed me a pamphlet on handling grief.

"...It helped me a lot when I lost my friend a long time ago. I'm sorry if it's crinkly and some of the colors are faded."

"Thanks so much. I'll check it out." I let him know. I didn't lie and read about grief in this pamphlet with outdated phone numbers, links and faded cartoons. *Sadly, it didn't help much and I returned it.*

Dr. Shirley's dismissal of my feelings and abrasive personality wasn't what I wanted or needed. I steered clear of her these couple weeks when reality set in and I spent lunch alone in the library. Nizhoni did try messaging a few times, but I didn't have the energy to see what she sent, so I just left her on *Delivered.* She would have stayed there indefinitely if she didn't come over tonight. I was sitting in my room, bundled in blankets watching a Youtube video about people moving to rural France. *Maladaptive daydreaming do your thing.*

Knock. Knock. Knock.

Erm. Nobody usually comes over and pounds on the door, especially at 8 P.M. I'm not getting out of bed–if it's an emergency they can call 911.

Knock. Knock. Knock.

Knock. Knock. Knock.

I'm not moving. This girl just bought an abandoned chateau in Nice. *Nice.*

Knock. Knock. Knock.

Knock. Knock. Knock.

Knock. Knock. Knock.

I hope whoever it is doesn't actually have an actual emergency.

Help! It's an emergency!

I heard this from my room, which was the farthest away from the front door. At this point, I was shaken up, but a little annoyed I was interrupted when I obviously was very busy. I unbundled myself and rushed to the door just in time to interrupt the knocks. I peeked through the curtains by the door and saw a crying Nizhoni. I wasn't ready for this and I was going to just lay back down then we made direct eye contact. Reluctantly, I acquiesced, knowing whatever resentment I feel can't outweigh whatever is making Nizhoni tremble.

"I'm sorry! I came over because you wouldn't respond. You were right. You didn't say anything but I'm sorry." Nizhoni said as she rushed through the door, landing a hug on my body.

"I was so stupid and I'm sorry. I'm sorry. *I'm sorry.*" Nizhoni said these words while gripping my body and forcing her way through tears. I no longer cared what happened between us because I missed her a lot, so tears gently streamed down my face as we reunited.

"It's fine. It's alright. What's wrong?" I inquired with a gentle tone trying to plant myself firmly in the moment.

"I couldn't do it anymore. He was so mean." Nizhoni cried even harder and her grip tightened.

"He was so mean and I'm so sorry."

"Me too." I responded, tightening my grip as well.

"I just can't. I can't." Nizhoni continued.

"I wish we didn't. I was so stupid. I don't know what to do."

"What do you mean? Is he bothering you?" I asked, trying to piece together what the last straw was.

"No, you're going to be mad." Nizhoni responded.

"Of course I won't be. We all mess up. Well, *we* mess up most of the time." I said, trying to comfort her.

"No, not this. It's bad, Rita. Bad…" Nizhoni let me know. I sighed because I felt like I knew where this was going.

"How long?" I asked.

"What do you mean?" Nizhoni asked as her grip loosened and we slowly fell to the ground, holding each other still.

"How many weeks?" I bluntly asked.

"I think 12." Nizhoni responded.

We didn't say much else that night. I could tell Nizhoni was oscillating through shame and sadness, wanting to dissipate into thin air. I let her sleep over that night, which Mom and Grams were very happy with. I kept reminding her that everything was going to be alright.

XI: Nizhóní?

The next couple weeks were just as foggy as the last. Nizhoni's eyes sunk deep into herself. Her eyes were retreating and hiding from everyone— even herself. What once were, well, strong and healthy almonds, have now become deeply burrowed with regret. She became my main concern, interrupting any thought I had about school and anyone else. Albuquerque was the closest place we could think of that had a Planned Parenthood. Or in our case, *Unplanned Parenthood*. I made that joke to Nizhoni and she told me that I was sick in the head. I hope my *adroit wit* reaches its target audience. No? Ok. Our planning took two weeks and we decided the best time to go would be early November. Hiccups in our planning were surprisingly few: being Navajo meant we were technically residents of New Mexico, so we had access to subsidized costs for the services we needed. We covered the rest by using https://www.plannedparenthood.org which gave helpful directories to funding opportunities. Minors in New Mexico don't need to inform their parents about seeking services from Planned Parenthood, but some other states require notarized documents from legal guardians. We embarked on a Saturday morning, having done consultations in Gallup already and doing our prerequisites the weeks before. We took my grandma's car, which didn't need a lot of explaining other than me saying that it was an "absolute emergency."

Leaving Window Rock in the morning at sunrise helped alleviate a lot of the stress we felt. The exaggerated red waves of the morning sky gave us a much needed sense of solace.

"I'm nervous." Nizhoni said groggily.

"It's ok to be nervous. Trepidation is the only appropriate response." I affirmed.

"What does trepidation mean?" Nizhoni asked.

"It means you *trepidate*." I said jokingly, which was enough for her to chuckle this early in the morning.

We didn't say much on the ride. The silence helped us process what our lives had become and what we hoped they would be. I didn't interrupt Nizhoni while she slept most of the 3 hour drive. It was a lot easier for me to focus on the ride and what trials we needed to face. Riley had gotten under Nizhoni's skin. He wouldn't leave her alone after she dumped him, but lately he's gotten worse. The constant harassment through text and him trying to flaunt his rebound only made things harder for Nizhoni. She never told him that she was pregnant. I understood because that made *'everything'* a lot easier for her to handle. I think her secrecy helped prevent it from seeming like reality. Her mother on the other hand didn't pry into her life. Nizhoni said that Sharice spent so much of her time moping and barely waking up for work at Bashas'. That made me angry. Her disregard of what her *"love of her life"* took from everyone else was exceedingly selfish. My mind has been so preoccupied with helping Nizhoni that the grief I had dealt with was placed on the backburner. I think that helping her was my way of coping. Mrs. Shirley asked me why I stopped seeing her at lunch, and tried to convince me to continue the tradition. I told her that I was busy trying to improve my grades for colleges, which she accepted halfheartedly.

"Thank you, Rita." Nizhoni said sometime on the outskirts of Albuquerque as we were driving along Route 66.

"Of course. I'm here." I let her know.

"No, for not ratting me out." She returned.

"What do you mean? If you don't want to tell Sharice then that's fine but Riley can eat a d—" was all I was able to state before she finished her thought.

"No, for not ratting me out to Dr. Shirley. Rosa told me." Nizhoni had let me know.

"What. How?" I asked.

"She heard you two arguing. I'm sorry for causing that. I lied to her too. I should've just told her." Nizhoni replied.

"It's okay. It wasn't my place." I comforted her.

The drive was long and slow. We barely arrived for our appointment with a 10 minute buffer. As we drove up to the building in a plaza along San Mateo, we could see a variety of protestors holding up signs. Most looked intimidating except a child holding up a sign that read "*Jezus loves babies.*"

"Oh, my god. We can't go in there!" Nizhoni exclaimed anxiously.

"It'll be fine. They're just protesting, and hey, there's a couple of people protesting their protest. It's *protest-ception.*" I explained.

"Let's just turn around. I can't let these people see me." Nizhoni elaborated her concern.

"It's alright. Nobody here knows you. They're just signs." I tried to alleviate her anxiety.

We got out of the chidí, which directed a lot of the attention on us. The anti-choice protesters couldn't approach outside of what security would let them. So they resorted to yelling bible verses and names. You can guess what the names were by playing mental hangman: S _ _ T and W_ O _E. Nizhoni looked dejected but I did my best to shield her and walk with her to the door. The protestations of the group intensified and they decided to migrate closer, which led to the pro-choice group to act as a line of defense. One man slid passed and got in our faces. He wouldn't relent even when we tried to go around him. Nizhoni was on the verge of tears. To redirect attention, I exclaimed the first thing I could think of.

"It's okay everybody! She's keeping this one! God bless!" I said with the most convincing smile I could muster.

"I am?" Nizhoni asked in a quiet confusion, which luckily the middle aged man that was blocking our path didn't catch. The two groups moved away from us and the door, arguing between each other closer to the sidewalk instead.

"No, but they don't need to know that." I said pushing the door straight open with no problems.

Checking in was simple and only really needed an ID for Nizhoni. We brought all of the required documents. Everything was going well and the environment made us feel comfortable. That was mostly because we love pink and everything there was pink. *Forget legally blonde, let's be chronically blonde.* We completed everything we had to, saying *'no'* to a tipping screen when the desk person turned around the screen for Nizhoni to sign. Nizhoni wanted to leave 15% but I pressed no without hesitation. We waited, sitting next to two older women in the waiting room. They looked like they were comforting each other just as Nizhoni and I were. They went to their appointment first until Nizhoni was finally called.

"Rita. I don't want to go alone." Nizhoni told me.

"You won't be. I'm right here." I let her know as she followed the doctor, turning around to look at me as she went into the room.

I fell asleep, being awoken by a Doctor and Nizhoni who was seemingly calm. The details slip my mind about what she told us in the next few minutes, but I wouldn't share them anyway because of a *HIPPO* violation. The Doctor's magnanimous words and farewell helped us feel reassured in our decision. We left happier and Nizhoni's eyes seemed much less burdened than before. The drive home would be just as long so we got gas in Nob Hill right before we left. The car ride was more pleasant and we played songs by Mariah Carey, Lana Del Rey and Fiona Apple. I've never felt happier singing along to a song called *Sullen Girl*. The ride home was near sunset and the day ended just as beautifully red as it started.

"Rita?" Nizhoni said to capture my attention.

"Yes, Duchess of Duke City." I joked.

"I'm sorry," she said.

"Don't be." I informed her.

The rest of the car ride could've been silent but I didn't want it to be.

"I was supposed to watch the Barbie movie with John that night." There was no gracious way of sharing the tidbit. Nizhoni's eyes widened then calmly fell.

"I'm sorry. Why didn't you tell me?" Nizhoni asked.

"I didn't want it to be true and telling someone else meant that it was." Was my best rationale for the situation.

"Riley and I did '*the deed*' before he said that he loved me…"

There was a brief moment of pause until Nizhoni finished with an important question.

"Rita, are we going to be ok?" Nizhoni asked.

"I hope so. I hope so…" is all I could give in reassurance.

FIN.

I don't know what I did to deserve all of the blessings I've been given. The beautiful part is—none of them have to last forever. I'm just lucky they lasted at all.

Sequel August 1st. Thanks, everyone ;)